ROCKY

Based on *The Railway Series* by the Rev. W. Awdry

Illustrations by
Robin Davies and Jerry Smith

EGMONT

EGMONT

We bring stories to life

First published in Great Britain 2007
by Egmont UK Limited
239 Kensington High Street, London W8 6SA

Thomas the Tank Engine & Friends™

A BRITT ALLCROFT COMPANY PRODUCTION

Based on The Railway Series by The Reverend W Awdry
© 2007 Gullane (Thomas) LLC. A HIT Entertainment Company

Thomas the Tank Engine & Friends and Thomas & Friends are trademarks of Gullane (Thomas) Limited.
Thomas the Tank Engine & Friends and Design is Reg. US. Pat. & Tm. Off.

HiT entertainment

ISBN 978 1 4052 3149 7
1 3 5 7 9 10 8 6 4 2
Printed in Great Britain

The Forest Stewardship Council (FSC) is an international, non-governmental organisation
dedicated to promoting responsible management of the world's forests. FSC operates a
system of forest certification and product labelling that allows consumers to identify
wood and wood-based products from well-managed forests.

For more information about Egmont's paper-buying policy please visit www.egmont.co.uk/ethicalpublishing

For more information about the FSC please visit their website at www.fsc.uk.org

*T*his is a story about Rocky, a new crane who is so big that he needs an engine to pull him. Edward and Gordon thought he was no use – until they really needed his help . . .

Edward is a Really Useful Engine. He has worked on The Fat Controller's Railway for many years.

One morning, he steamed into the Docks to pick up some heavy pipes. Gordon and Thomas were already there, talking about a new crane called Rocky who had just arrived on the Island.

"He looks so strong!" Thomas puffed excitedly. "I'm sure he could lift even you up, Gordon!"

Gordon sniffed.

"That crane might be big," he said. "But he has no engine! He can't move unless one of us pulls him!"

Edward looked at the crane and saw that Gordon was right.

"Then I don't think he can be Really Useful," chuffed Edward, slowly.

"Quite right, Edward," huffed Gordon. "He will only get in the way!"

Just then, Percy arrived. He was very excited to see the new crane!

"He will only get in the way," huffed Edward.

"New-fangled nonsense!" Gordon wheeshed. And he chuffed off.

"What's a new-funnelled nuisance, Edward?" peeped Percy.

"New-fangled nonsense, Percy!" puffed Edward, as grandly as he could. "It's something that is new and not Really Useful."

Edward's trucks were right by the new crane.

"My name's Rocky," the crane smiled at Edward.

"I'm Edward," puffed the blue engine.

"Can I come with you?" asked Rocky. "I could help you with those heavy pipes."

"I don't need your help," sniffed Edward. "New-fangled nonsense!"

And he puffed off quickly . . . before the pipes had been properly tied down!

Edward was approaching a signal. He was going too fast, but he was so busy thinking about Rocky that he didn't notice.

Suddenly the signal changed to red!

Edward screeched to a stop. He jolted his trucks so much that their sides collapsed. Steel pipes toppled all over the tracks!

"Bust my buffers!" puffed Edward.

Edward looked at the heavy pipes and wondered if Rocky might help him lift them. Thomas had said the new crane was very strong.

"New-fangled nonsense!" huffed Edward.

He asked his Driver to telephone for Harvey instead. Soon the crane steamed up and started moving the pipes. But they were so heavy that he could only lift them one by one.

"This is going to take me a very long time," poor Harvey gasped.

Just then, Thomas and Emily arrived. They stopped and looked at the pipes.

"We have to get through!" tooted Thomas. "Why don't you go and get Rocky?"

"No, no!" whistled Edward. "Harvey is doing a fine job. We must be patient!"

"I don't like being patient!" pouted Emily. "We have a very important job to do!"

Then they heard Gordon coming.

Gordon was rushing along very fast. He tried to stop when he saw the pipes, but it was too late. He hit them with a loud crunch, and came off the track!

It was a terrible mess. Gordon lay groaning in a pile of broken pipes.

"I can't lift Gordon!" sighed Harvey. "He's too heavy!"

"Edward!" tooted Thomas. "We need Rocky!"

Gordon looked up. "New-fangled nonsense!" he sniffed.

But Edward knew this was a disaster! Harvey couldn't possibly lift Gordon.

There was only one thing to do.

"I'll go and get Rocky!" Edward wheeshed, and raced off.

Edward steamed back to the Docks.

"Rocky, we need your help," he whistled. "It's an emergency!"

"I'm ready and waiting, Edward!" cried Rocky, happily.

So Edward buffered up to Rocky, and together they left for the junction.

Everyone cheered as Edward pulled Rocky up hills and down valleys. He felt very proud to be pulling the newest arrival on Sodor.

Edward soon pulled up beside Gordon, bringing Rocky to help.

"I can fix this!" promised Rocky, smiling.

With his mighty crane arm, he lifted Gordon back on to the track.

Gordon was very surprised.

"Thank you, Rocky!" he huffed. "Good work!"

Then Rocky lifted all the pipes off the rails.

The job was done in no time!

Gordon and Edward were very impressed.

"I was silly to call you 'new-fangled nonsense'," wheeshed Edward to Rocky. "You might be new, but you're also Really Useful. Welcome to our Island!"

Everyone tooted and cheered for Rocky!

The Thomas Story Library is THE definitive collection of stories about Thomas and ALL his friends.

There are now 50 stories
from the Island of Sodor
to collect!

So go on, start your Thomas Story Library NOW!

A Fantastic Offer for Thomas the Tank Engine Fans!

In every Thomas Story Library book like this one, you will find a special token. Collect 6 Thomas tokens and we will send you a brilliant Thomas poster, and a double-sided bedroom door hanger! Simply tape a £1 coin in the space above, and fill out the form overleaf.

TO BE COMPLETED BY AN ADULT

To apply for this great offer, ask an adult to complete the coupon below and send it with a pound coin and 6 tokens, to:
THOMAS OFFERS, PO BOX 715, HORSHAM RH12 5WG

☐ Please send a Thomas poster and door hanger. I enclose 6 tokens plus a £1 coin. (Price includes P&P)

Fan's name...

Address...

....Postcode...........................

Date of birth...

Name of parent/guardian...

Signature of parent/guardian...